The Nantucket Lightship Basket Mystery

Carolyn Carmody
illustrated by Samantha Bell

**for
Jeff and Jeffrey**

Special thanks to Laura Backus of CBI
for her advice and direction

Table of Contents

Nantucket!

Erin's heart skipped a beat as the ferry pulled into Steamboat Wharf. She could hardly believe she was back on Nantucket, the place where she was born! Cottages, stores, yachts, and church steeples all nestled together like sun-baked cookies fresh out of the oven. She waved at the crowd of people waiting on the wharf for the approaching ferry. Seagulls circling overhead kept an eye out for morsels of food tossed onto the pier.

Suddenly Erin spied a tall, trim woman on the wharf. "There she is! There's Aunt Kate!" she exclaimed to her best friend, Jacob.

A month earlier, Erin's great aunt had invited her to spend some time on Nantucket Island, off the coast of Massachusetts. "I'd like you to see the Harbor House Hotel where your mother and father used to work, because this is the last summer it will be open," Aunt Kate had told Erin on the phone. "Your Uncle Dave's the manager, so you'll get one of the best rooms. Plus, you can come to the award ceremony honoring me for my philanthropy on the island. Imagine getting an award for helping out the community I love!" Erin had searched her brain for a good excuse not to go. Spending part of her summer in an old hotel with her relatives didn't sound all that exciting. Then Aunt Kate had added, "Bring a friend!" Erin pictured her and Jacob lying on the beach while Aunt Kate went to one of her endless meetings. *That might actually be fun*, she thought.

"Welcome to Nantucket!" exclaimed Aunt Kate after Erin and Jacob clattered down the gangway and stepped into the waiting area below. She set down the honey-colored basket with a lid she was carrying and gave Erin a big hug. Then she turned to Jacob and hugged him. "Erin has told me all about you," Aunt Kate said, her blue eyes sparkling. "I'm so happy you could come!"

"I'm happy to be here," said Jacob. "Thank you for inviting me!" He reached into his pocket and pulled out a pair of binoculars. "I brought these along so I could check out all the cool stuff on Nantucket, like the whales. And I plan on taking lots of pictures for a scrapbook of Nantucket while we're here!" he said, tapping the camera hanging around his neck.

Erin rolled her eyes. "Jacob wants to be a pho[to]journalist and he's never happy unless he's taking pictur[es] with his new digital camera."

Aunt Kate smiled at Jacob. "You'd have to go out in [a] whale-watching boat to see a live whale," she said, "but y[ou] can learn a lot at the Whaling Museum here on the island."

Aunt Kate squeezed Erin's shoulder. "Your Unc[le] Dave will be happy to see you, Erin. He remembers wh[en] your father and mother worked at the Harbor House befo[re] your mother died and you were still a baby." She picked [up] the basket with one hand and one of Erin's bags with t[he] other, then quickly led the way through the crowded pier t[o a] cobblestoned street. "I hope you both remembered to bri[ng] clothes for the awards ceremony on Saturday. They're calli[ng] my award *Excellence in Service to Nantucket*. I'm glad you t[wo] will be there, but we must dress the part!"

4

Jacob leaned close to Erin. "Will there be food at this ceremony?" he whispered.

Erin shrugged. "I think so. It's in some sort of fancy restaurant. It means a lot to Aunt Kate, so act like you're really excited about going."

Jacob smiled. "I always find food exciting."

"Here we are." Aunt Kate turned into an entrance way with townhouses on one side and cottages and a swimming pool on the other. At the end of the way stood a building with the words HARBOR HOUSE in large letters across the front. Erin recognized the hotel from the pictures her father had shown her. Suddenly she felt as if she were coming home!

A man with short, straight black hair and a big sm

came through the front door toward them.

"There's Uncle Dave!" cried Erin. She gave her und

a big hug before he turned to Jacob.

"You must be Jacob," Uncle Dave said, giving Jacob

firm handshake. "Welcome to the Harbor House!"

Erin looked around the lobby at the elegant drapes hanging from windows and paintings of ships and seacoasts adorning the walls. A sign by the front-desk said *"Welcome to the Harbor House—1902-2007."*

She was happy she was getting to see the Harbor House before it closed.

Uncle Dave introduced them to Jane, the front-desk manager. She wore earrings in the shape of Nantucket.

"It's so nice to meet you!" Jane said with a smile. "Kate has been telling everyone you were coming!"

A younger woman standing behind the front desk looked up briefly and smiled at Erin—then went back to checking in a woman with two young boys. A second desk worker glanced up from her computer but didn't smile before returning to her work. Erin had the strange feeling the woman didn't like her.

"This is Mary Fox," said Jane pointing to the young woman checking in the woman and two boys. "And this is Mary Smith." Jane pointed to the second desk clerk working at the computer. "Since they're both named Mary, we call them Mary F and Mary S so we can tell them apart." She smiled at the two clerks.

"Hi, Mary F and Mary S!" said Jacob.

Erin glanced at a girl about her age sitting in a chair near the front desk. The girl glared at Erin and then looked away.

"I'll show you your rooms now," said Aunt Kate. "They're right next to mine. Then I have to run to a meeting of the Arts Council. Jane is going to give you a tour of the Harbor House grounds and take a walk with you downtown so you can see some more of Nantucket. I'll meet you at six o'clock for dinner at the Hearth Restaurant."

The Harbor House Robbery

Erin and Jacob sat in the Hearth Restaurant acro[ss] the lobby from the front desk of the Harbor House. Erin r[an] her hands over the white tablecloth and looked across t[he] room at the baby grand piano. "This is like a restaurant we [go] to for special holidays," she said to Jacob. "But the ho[tel] guests get to eat here every day."

"Uncle Dave has a very nice hotel," said Jacob. "Wh[at] will he do after it closes?"

"Uncle Dave will have his pick of jobs," said Er[in]. "He's a great hotel manager. The people he works with a[nd] the people on the island love him. He's already had o[ne]

10

interview for the manager position at the Grey Whale Hotel that will open up at the end of the summer."

"Aunt Kate said she's been visiting friends for the last three days," said Jacob. "She must have a lot of friends on the island if she's been visiting all that time." He watched as a waitress brought the order for a couple with two young children sitting at the table next to them.

"She does," said Erin. "She was born on Nantucket and lived here until she left to go to college. Then she got married and moved to Boston. She and her husband made a lot of money, and that's how she became a philanthropist."

"A what?"

"A philanthropist. That's a person who gives lots of money to good causes. Aunt Kate has donated to the Arts Council and other organizations on the island for a long time. That's why she's being honored at the awards ceremony

11

Saturday. Aunt Kate really loves Nantucket and comes back whenever she can to visit."

"Hey, I'd come back to visit whenever I could, too," said Jacob, "if I could have more of that fudge we got on our walk with Jane this afternoon. It was great!"

"I'll be right back," said Erin. "I want to make sure Aunt Kate's not waiting for us in the lobby." She looked out the door of the restaurant and saw a man sitting on a small couch reading a newspaper. A woman with bushy blond hair was hovering around the front desk. *There's something weird about that woman*, thought Erin. Then she shrugged and returned to the restaurant.

"Jane must really like those baskets with lids like Aunt Kate has because she talked about how beautiful they were every time she saw one in a store window," Jacob said when Erin sat down. "I liked the designs they had on their lids."

"They're called lightship baskets," said Erin. "The basket Aunt Kate has was my mother's. She asked Aunt Kate to keep it for me before she died, and give it to me when I turn sixteen. Lightship baskets usually have a decoration out of whalebone or ivory set in the lid."

Aunt Kate joined Erin and Jacob for dinner, and by dessert she had given them a short history of Nantucket. And she told them about growing up on the island and stargazing with friends through the Maria Mitchell Observatory telescopes, picking blueberries, and making shell bracelets. Lost in Aunt Kate's stories, Erin forgot her worries about being bored on the island.

Erin pulled a portfolio from under her chair and handed it to Aunt Kate. "I brought these pictures to show you," she said. "I thought you might enjoy seeing them."

"Erin's a great artist," said Jacob. "She can draw ju[st] about anything! I can draw a robot with two heads. Tha[t] about it."

Erin grinned at Jacob while Aunt Kate studied t[he] drawings of animals and children. "These are lovely," s[he] said. "Jane's good friend, Peter Anderson, owns Isla[nd] Gallery on Main Street and is a member of the Arts Coun[cil] on Nantucket. He's having a children's art show in his galle[ry] this summer. He might be interested in these drawings for t[he] show. You could stop by the gallery and see what he says."

"I've never been in a gallery show!" Erin sa[id] excitedly. She flipped the pages of her portfolio. "Hm[m,] there's one more picture I wanted to show you. It must s[till] be in my room." She hopped out of her chair. "I'll be rig[ht] back."

"Could you grab my camera while you're up there?" Jacob asked. He pointed to the slices of blueberry pie the waitresses were setting on the table. "Those are humongous. I need to take a picture for my scrapbook. I think I'll have a section called *Giant Foods of Nantucket*!"

Erin ran up the stairs to her room and took the drawing of a girl riding a horse out of her suitcase. Then she found Jacob's camera on his bed in his room. After locking the door, she was hurrying down the hallway studying her picture when she ran smack into a woman entering Aunt Kate's room with a large stack of towels. Both Erin and the woman fell onto the plush green carpet.

"Oh! I'm so sorry!" exclaimed Erin. The woman's bushy blond hair stuck up from her head and her dark sunglasses had slipped down her nose. She brushed off the front of her black pantsuit and reached for a sandal that had

flipped off her foot. Erin picked up Jacob's camera and stared at the woman's toes. She wished she could take a picture of them. They were big enough to be in a section of Jacob's scrapbook called *Giant Hairy Toes of Nantucket*!

"I'm so sorry," Erin said again. She started to hand the woman her towels but the woman began sneezing. After sneezing three times in a row, the woman scooped up the towels, unlocked the door to Aunt Kate's room, hurried in and locked the door behind her. *Do I know her?* Erin thought. *She looks familiar.*

"Here I am," said Erin, sliding back into her chair. She gave Jacob his camera. Then she looked at Aunt Kate and handed her the picture. "I ran into a housekeeper going into your room with a large stack of towels."

"That's strange," said Aunt Kate. "I didn't request an towels."

Jacob took a picture of his pie and everyone at dessert. "I'm stuffed," said Aunt Kate, dabbing crumbs o the corner of her mouth. "I've got an unexpected meeting 'Sconset in the morning, but why don't we meet back here noon for lunch, and then we can bike around the island?" S yawned. "Can you two occupy yourselves this evening? I' exhausted."

"Sure," Erin said. "Uncle Dave offered to take us the Boat Basin when he gets off work tonight. See yo tomorrow!"

Erin and Jacob sat in the lobby waiting for Unc Dave, when suddenly Aunt Kate ran down the stairs. "T lightship basket is missing!" she exclaimed.

Peeping Toms

Erin and Jacob stayed in the lobby while Aunt Kate and Uncle Dave talked to the police officer in Aunt Kate's room.

"I'm sorry your mother's lightship basket was stolen, Erin," said Jacob. He twiddled with the fringe on a pillow that matched the upholstery of the couch. "I'm sure the police will find the thief and get it back."

"Thanks, Jacob," said Erin. A tear ran down her face. "My mother's lightship basket is the only thing I have that my mother gave just to me. She even put a letter inside the basket saying how much she loved me and how much she wished she could see me grow up. Having the basket stolen feels li[ke] my mother died all over again." She pulled a Kleenex from [the] box on a small table near the couch and blew her nose.

"Why would someone want to steal it?" said Jacob.

"It's a family heirloom," said Erin. "It was passe[d] down from my mother's grandmother, to her mother, ar[d] then to her. It was made by Jose Reyes and is worth a lot [of] money."

"Who's Jose Reyes?" said Jacob.

"Jose Reyes was a very talented and famous lightsh[ip] basket maker who came to live on Nantucket in the 1940s[," said Erin. "People came from everywhere to buy lightsh[ip] baskets from him, but since so many people wanted basket[s,] they sometimes had to wait two to three years to get one."

"Wow!" exclaimed Jacob. "That's a long time to w[ait] for a purse!"

Jacob picked up a scrapbook lying on the small table with the words THE HARBOR HOUSE—1902–2007 on the cover. "The Harbor House sure looks different now from when it was first built," he said, flipping through the pages in the book, "and so do the people from back then." He pointed to a news release attached to an old newspaper clipping about the Harbor House. "Hey, these people got something stolen just like you," he said.

Erin read the news release aloud.

REWARD OFFERED

The Smith family is offering a reward for information leading to the arrest and conviction of the intruder responsible for the theft of a small safe containing a substantial amount of cash and jewelry from their residence at 18 India Street the night of June 20,

1952, while they were away. The Smith family asks anyone who might have seen an intruder entering or leaving their residence on the night of June 20, 1952, to please contact them.

"Wow!" said Erin. "I wonder if they ever got it bac That address sounds familiar." She pulled her attention aw from the scrapbook and jumped off the couch. "Come c Jacob!" she said. "We're wasting time!"

"Wasting time?"

"We've got to look for clues while the crime is s hot! I want my mother's lightship basket back and I'm goi to find the thief who stole it!" She paused for a minute. wonder how many keys there are for each room."

They checked with the clerk at the front desk.

"There are three keys for each room," said the college student who worked evenings. "We usually give the guest one key and keep the other two for backup."

"Excuse me," he said. "I need to take some towels to a room." He put a sign on the desk that said *Back in a Minute*, went into an office behind the front desk and left carrying a stack of towels.

As soon as he'd left the lobby, Erin walked around the corner and pushed open the door to the small office behind the front desk. A lamp on a desk lit the room. A computer and a stack of papers sat on another desk.

Erin motioned to Jacob to follow her. "Look," she said, pointing to a long, thin metal box hanging on the wall. "There are the keys." The door to the box was ajar. Inside keys hung on pegs in room number order.

"It would be easy as pie to take a key out of this b[ox]

when no one was looking," said Jacob.

"There are two keys to Aunt Kate's room here," sa[id]

Erin. "And she has one. That makes three keys. It looks li[ke]

all the keys are accounted for."

Erin led the way out of the small office and down t[he]

stairs to the basement. "The housekeeper must have come [up]

the stairs from the basement because that's whe[re]

housekeeping is. My father told me that."

"It's spooky down here!" said Jacob when th[ey]

reached the basement. He tried to open the door mark[ed]

Housekeeping but it was locked.

Erin looked at the stacks of towels on a bench by t[he]

housekeeping door. "Those towels look like the ones t[he]

housekeeper dropped when I ran into her."

24

"They smell sweet," said Jacob, bending down to smell them. "They must wash them in perfumey smelling soap. They make me want to sneeze."

Erin remembered the housekeeper sneezing after she knocked her down. "I think they might have made the housekeeper I ran into sneeze," she said.

Erin and Jacob returned to the lobby just as Uncle Dave, Aunt Kate, and a police officer came downstairs. Aunt Kate blew her nose and dabbed her eyes with Kleenex. "I'm so sorry, Erin," she said. "I can't imagine who would want to steal your mother's lightship basket."

Uncle Dave ran his fingers through his short hair as if he were trying to solve a problem but couldn't. "Whoever stole the basket had to have a key to open the door," he said, "but I called Jane and she said she hadn't given out any extra keys to Aunt Kate's room."

Erin jumped up. "Remember I told you I saw

housekeeper going into your room carrying towels when

went upstairs during dinner?" she said to Aunt Kate.

"What did the housekeeper look like?" asked t

policeman.

Erin didn't have to think very hard. She could still s

the woman sitting on the carpet surrounded by towels. "S

had bushy blond hair and was wearing a black suit and bla

sandals and dark sunglasses," she said.

"Do you remember anything else?" asked t

policeman.

"Actually, she had bushy brown hair on her toes," sa

Erin. She closed her eyes. "Oh, now I remember! I saw her

the front desk before Aunt Kate came down for dinner."

"We don't have any housekeepers with bushy blo

hair," said Uncle Dave, "and the front desk takes care

room service in the evening. There *was* a pile of towels in Aunt Kate's room," he continued. "It looks like the thief picked up a pile of towels that was supposed to go to the pool and used them so she'd look like she was from room service."

"I need some information from you, young lady," said the policeman, looking at Erin. "You may have been a witness to a crime."

After she finished talking to the policeman, Erin ran upstairs and knocked on Jacob's door. When there was no answer, she gently opened the door and found Jacob asleep on his bed. "Wake up! Jacob, wake up!" she exclaimed and shook his shoulder until he swung his feet over the side of the bed and sat up.

"What! What happened?"

"Since Uncle Dave didn't get to take us to the Bo
Basin, he gave me some money for us to get ice cream— ju
so we're back by dark. We could look for the thief while we'
out. Her bushy blond hair would be hard to miss!"

"If I'm going to be a detective, then I'd better
prepared," said Jacob. He grabbed his camera and follow
Erin out the door.

"What did the policeman ask you?" said Jacob as th
headed out the back door of the Harbor House toward tow

"He just wanted to know what happened when I we
upstairs and saw the woman going into Aunt Kate's room
said Erin. "I told him everything I could remember. T
news release about the theft will be in the paper tomorrow.'

Erin stepped off the sidewalk to let a woman pushi
a stroller with twins in it go by as they walked down a str

filled with summer tourists. She tried to take her mind off the missing basket by looking at a pretty sundress with dolphins on it on a mannequin in the window of a shop. Another mannequin wore a pair of baggy shorts and a top to match. Erin couldn't imagine wearing such baggy shorts. They looked as if they were going to fall off the mannequin!

She and Jacob walked around a line of people in colorful shorts, swim suits, and even dressy dresses in front of a restaurant called Papa's Pizza.

"That smells good!" said Jacob.

"It sure does," said Erin. She got a whiff of something coming from another restaurant, but it didn't smell that good at all.

"I wonder how the thief knew Aunt Kate would be in the Hearth Restaurant at six o'clock?" said Jacob.

Erin looked at Jacob. "That's a good question," she said. "You *are* a detective!" She thought a moment. "Maybe one of the desk clerks heard us talking about meeting for dinner and told the thief."

"That would make her an accomplice to the crime," Jacob exclaimed.

Erin saw some bushy blond hair but it belonged to a young girl riding on a man's shoulders.

"That's right!" said Erin. "I don't think it would have been Mary F," she said. "She seemed nice. But maybe it could have been the other desk clerk, Mary S. She didn't look too friendly when Jane introduced her."

"Or, maybe it was Uncle Dave or Jane since they were both there when Aunt Kate said she'd meet us for dinner," said Jacob.

"I definitely don't think Uncle Dave had anything to do with my mother's missing basket," said Erin. She couldn't imagine her favorite uncle helping someone steal her mother's basket. "Maybe it was Jane."

"Hey, look at that!" Jacob pointed to a restaurant sign that said BROTHERHOOD OF THIEVES hanging on a white clapboard building. Through the windows candles flickered and a long line of people stood waiting to enter the restaurant. "That deserves a picture!"

He grabbed the camera hanging from around his neck and clicked a picture. Then he enlarged the image on his camera's view screen.

"Look," he said. "There's someone with bushy blond hair at the front of the line of people waiting to go into the restaurant!"

31

Erin glanced up the line. "You're right," she exclaimed. "And they just went into the restaurant. Let's get line and see if it's the same lady I saw going into Aunt Kate room! If it is maybe we can solve the crime tonight!"

"I didn't bring any money," said Jacob. "And anyw; we'd have to wait in line a long time to get in."

"That's true," said Erin. She noticed the manicure hedge that grew along the side of the building. "Maybe w can crawl through that hedge and look through the window she said.

Erin stood on her tiptoes on a rock ledge that r around the side of the building and peered through a windc The restaurant was dark inside except for the light comi from candles. Erin could see waiters and waitresses walki around and people sitting at tables talking and eating.

"I see something that looks bushy," said Jacob, standing on the ledge in front of the window next to Erin. "Only it's kind of hard to tell what it is."

"Where?" said Erin.

"It's at a table up near the front of the room."

Erin wiped the dust off the window glass, stood on her tiptoes again, and pressed her nose against the window. Suddenly she saw a man and a woman peering back at her!

The woman waved! Erin fell backwards off the ledge and landed in the hedge.

"Ouch!" she said. She got to her feet and brushed clump of mud off her knee.

"What's the matter?" asked Jacob from his perch the ledge.

"We'd better get out of here. Some people saw r looking in the window! Aunt Kate would be embarrassed death if she thought we were Peeping Toms!"

"May I help you?" A waiter wearing a bandana and large, round earring looked down at Erin and Jacob as th crawled through an opening in the hedge.

"We wanted to see if someone was in the restauran said Erin. "We didn't mean to disturb anyone." She hoped t man would not report them to the police or call the Harl House.

"Why don't you come inside the restaurant and take a look around?" said the waiter. "It would probably be easier that way."

"That person with the bushy blond hair we saw going into the restaurant was definitely not the person I saw going into Aunt Kate's room, and I think the thing you saw through the window was a plant," said Erin as she and Jacob walked down the street.

"Yeah, I know," said Jacob. "But, it was a bushy plant."

Erin looked at the darkening sky. "Last one back to the Harbor House is a pigeon-toed pirate!"

Is This the Missing Basket?

The next morning Erin stood in line with Jacob and other Harbor House guests at the breakfast buffet in the Hearth Restaurant. She thought of her mother's missing lightship basket and the housekeeper with the bushy blond hair.

"It's up to us to find the thief and get my mother's lightship basket back," she said when she and Jacob returned to their table. "I know the police aren't going to have time to walk around Nantucket looking for someone with bushy blond hair and hairy toes. And we can't get anyone else help us, because the police told me to keep what I saw to myself for now."

She poured syrup on her pancakes and then handed the bottle to Jacob. "Since we don't meet Aunt Kate until noon for lunch, I think the first thing we should do is walk downtown and look for someone with bushy blond hair again," she said. "There can't be too many people with hair like that walking around on Nantucket and she should be easier to spot in broad daylight. If we see someone with bushy blond hair and she's the same size as the thief, we can follow her and see if she has hairy toes." She paused and thanked the waitress for filling her juice glass. "Then we can go to the Atheneum and get some information about the organizations Aunt Kate donated to over the years, because I want to give a short presentation when she receives her award. And I also want to get some information about th Delaney family here on Nantucket."

"What's the Atheneum and who are the Delaneys said Jacob.

"The Atheneum is the library here on Nantucke said Erin. "Delaney was my mother's last name before s married my father. She grew up on Nantucket just like Au Kate. I want to see if I can find some information about h family and maybe a clue about why someone would want steal the lightship basket she gave me."

"Sounds like a good idea to me," said Jacob. I poured more syrup on his pancakes. "Just let me finish the pancakes. Detectives need fuel."

Erin and Jacob bumped smack into two policeme leaving Uncle Dave's office when they went to tell him whe they were going.

Uncle Dave motioned for Erin and Jacob to come into his office and have a seat. "Did they find the thief?" asked Erin excitedly.

"No, they didn't, I'm sorry to say," said Uncle Dave. "They were here to tell me I've been accused of stealing diamonds and other jewelry from a guest on the third floor."

"Oh, no!" exclaimed Erin.

"The lady on the third floor asked me to come in and look at the air conditioner in her room yesterday evening," he said. "I saw a lot of jewelry on a dresser when I went in the room. The lady said she would be out for the evening." He took a drink from a mug of coffee on his desk. "I told her I would get the part the air conditioner needed and put it in while she was gone."

"After the police left last night I went back up to the lady's room and put the new part in the air conditioner." He ran his fingers through his hair. "The jewelry was still on the dresser. After I left her room I worked at the front desk until you guys came back from your walk downtown. Then I went home and went to bed."

He took another drink from the mug and set it down. "I never touched the jewelry. The lady says the jewelry was gone when she returned later in the evening. She thinks I stole the jewelry when I went back to put the part in her conditioner, but I didn't."

"Oh, no!" said Erin again. "What's going to happen now?"

"I don't know," said Uncle Dave. "I just know I didn't steal the jewelry and if the police find the jewelry they won't find my fingerprints on it because I never even touched it."

"Is there anything we can do to help?" said Jacob.

"Thanks for asking, Jacob," said Uncle Dave. "There's nothing you can do right now. Just go ahead and do what you both planned to do. I'll let you know if anything else develops."

"Why would anyone want to frame Uncle Dave?" said Erin as she and Jacob walked out the back door of the Harbor House toward town. She was more upset about Uncle Dave than she was about her missing basket. "He's a great hotel manager and tries to be nice to people."

"I don't know," said Jacob. "Maybe someone wants him to look bad."

"Maybe *she's* the thief." Jacob pointed at a young woman with blond hair walking up the street with a large black dog and eating an ice cream cone piled three scoo[ps]

high.

"She's too small and her hair isn't bushy enough," sa[id]

Erin.

"That ice cream cone sure looks good, and it's huge[,]"

said Jacob, and clicked a picture with his camera.

Main Street was full of people going in and out of shops a[nd]

restaurants.

"There's Island Gallery," said Erin, pointing to a sho[p]

on the opposite side of the street. "Let's stop by as Au[nt]

Kate suggested."

A man wearing a blue tie and stripped shirt w[as]

talking to a group of people across the room when Erin a[nd]

Jacob entered the gallery.

Erin glanced at the pleasing arrangement of pictures on the walls of the gallery. There were portraits of people and paintings of ships, landscapes, dogs, cats, and seagulls. Erin also noticed several large paintings signed by Peter Anderson on easels near the front of the gallery and some smaller versions of the paintings standing against the wall behind the front desk.

She walked over and picked up one of the smaller paintings. "My father would love one of these," she said, brushing her hand over the top of the painting. Suddenly the picture moved to the side revealing a small compartment built into the frame back.

"Here comes someone," said Jacob.

Erin quickly slid the picture back into place and stood the painting up against the wall.

"Welcome to Island Gallery," said the man wearing the blue tie and stripped shirt. "How may I help you?"

"We're looking for Mr. Peter Anderson," said Erin.

"At your service," said the man with a smile.

"I'm Erin Kelly and this is my friend, Jacob," Erin said. "We're visiting my great aunt, Kate Kelly, at the Harbor House. She said you might be interested in seeing some of my pictures for the children's art show you're having in your gallery this summer."

Just then the girl Erin had seen in the Harbor House lobby when they arrived came in the front door of the gallery.

"I'd like you to meet my niece, Adrienne Smith," said Peter. "Adrienne, this is Erin Kelly and her friend, Jacob. They're visiting Kate Kelly at the Harbor House."

Erin and Jacob both smiled and said "hello". Adrienne stretched her lips into a half smile, then walked behind the front desk and began stacking papers.

"I'd be happy to take a look at your pictures!" Peter Anderson continued. "I know your Aunt Kate well and consider her to be a good judge of art. I'll be in 'Sconset most of the day, but I need to stop by my house to pick u

some papers before I go. It's not far from the Harbor Hous

If you could get your pictures and meet me there in half a

hour that would be great!" he said. "Jane can give you t

address."

Peter drove up just as Erin and Jacob reached h

house. He got a key from under a statue on the porch a

opened the front door. He laid Erin's pictures on a ch

inside the door and picked up a stack of papers.

"I'm sorry I have to run," he said, "but I'm alrea

late." He locked the door and put the key back under t

statue.

"I'll look at your pictures as soon as I get back t

afternoon," he said and drove off.

Erin and Jacob made their way back to Main Street.

"Look!" Jacob pointed to a woman walking up the other side of the street. She had lots of bushy blond hair and was carrying a lightship basket and a large beach bag. "Maybe *she's* the thief."

"Her hair looks bushy enough," said Erin. "She's going into Mitchell's Book Corner. Quick! Let's follow her!"

Erin and Jacob hurried across Main Street to the bookstore. "I'll go in and see what decoration is on the lid. My mother's basket has an ivory whale on the lid." She pushed on the door to the bookstore. "Wait here at the front door in case she decides to leave."

Inside the main room of the store, books with colorful covers were displayed on shelves along the wall and on free-standing cases in the middle of the room. A mural of

books lying on a sandy beach wound around the walls ne

the ceiling. Erin promised herself she'd come back ar

browse when she had more time. She walked through tl

main room into the children's area. The lady with the busl

blond hair was sitting at the table reading a children's pictu

book. The lightship basket was sitting on the table by he

Erin made her way around a large stuffed kangaroo, glanc

at the basket and then left the store.

"The basket has a whale carving on top," said Erin when she joined Jacob in front of the bookstore.

"Yippee! That means we've found the basket!" exclaimed Jacob. "Let's call the police! Then we can go to the Atheneum and look up stuff. And then we can get on our bathing suits and hit the beach!"

"Not so fast!" said Erin. "There are lots of lightship baskets with a whale carving on the lid. But, I could definitely tell if the lightship basket was my mother's if I could see the bottom of it. Authentic Nantucket lightship baskets are made by hand and the artist always signs the bottom of the basket. My mother's basket has Jose Reyes's signature on the bottom of it and also a map of Nantucket and a small notch. I couldn't see the bottom of the basket because the lady had it sitting next to her on a table."

"What about her toes?" said Jacob. "Were they b
and hairy?"

"I couldn't see them," said Erin. "She's wearing tenr
shoes."

"Look, she's coming out of the bookstore," said Er
She and Jacob watched the woman turn right and walk dov
the sidewalk toward the waterfront. She had the lightsh
basket and the beach bag with her.

"Let's see where she goes," said Jacob. "I'll take
picture of her in case she's the thief." He clicked a picture
the woman looking through the windows of a shop.

The woman turned left at the bottom of Main Stre
"Look!" said Erin. "I bet she's going to the beach. Le
follow her. Maybe we can check the bottom of the basket!"

Swimming in the Basin

The woman took a towel out of the beach bag and spread it out on the sand at Children's Beach. Then she set the lightship basket and beach bag on it. All around people lay sunning themselves on brightly colored towels or walked in the water along the shore. Children with buckets and shovels built sandcastles in the wet sand near the water. Seagulls dove down from the brilliant blue sky to catch scraps of food thrown by generous souls.

The woman took a book and snack out of her beach bag. Erin and Jacob sat in the sand not far behind her and looked out at the ocean.

"Why do they call it a lightship basket?" asked Jacob.

"Because the first lightship baskets were made on lightship," said Erin. "That's a boat that acts like a floating lighthouse. They hung oil lamps in lanterns up on the mast of the lightships so ships passing by would see them and not crash into the shoals around Nantucket."

"What are shoals?" said Jacob. "And how do you know so much about Nantucket?"

"My mom's family is from here and so is my dad's, I've been hearing Nantucket history all my life. Shoals are kind of sandbar caused by currents in the ocean moving sand around underwater. If the current piles up sand in one place the water becomes shallow there and ships run aground. They watched as two girls tossed crackers to a seagull hovering overhead.

"Aunt Kate told me all about Jose Reyes and lightships when I visited her in Boston on my birthday two years ago. She only uses my mother's basket when she comes to Nantucket."

"Maybe Aunt Kate forgot and left it somewhere," said Jacob.

"I don't think so," said Erin. "She says she remembers leaving it in her room when she came down for dinner."

After a while the woman got up and walked toward the snack bar. "I'm going to check the bottom of her lightship basket," Erin said. "Tell me if she starts coming back this way." She quickly walked over to the woman's towel, picked up the lightship basket, and looked at the bottom.

"Well, that was a waste of time," she said when she plopped back on the sand next to Jacob. "It's not my mother's."

"Whoever stole your mother's lightship basket must have known Aunt Kate had it, and where she was staying," said Jacob. The woman was coming back from the snack bar carrying a large soda and a candy bar.

"Probably," Erin said. "But it wouldn't have had to be someone who knew Aunt Kate. It could have been anyone who saw her with it. It would have been easy to follow Aunt Kate back to the Harbor House."

"Or, maybe someone heard Aunt Kate was rich and decided to break into her room to steal something," said Jacob.

"That's a possibility, too," said Erin.

Soon the woman finished her candy bar and soda. She took off her tennis shoes, put the lightship basket in her beach bag, and began walking toward the water.

54

"I guess that lady is going to work off that candy bar she just ate," said Jacob. "I could use a candy bar myself about now," he added.

"You don't need a candy bar after all those pancakes you had for breakfast," said Erin. "I beat you by half a block getting back to the Harbor House last night!"

"That's because you cheated!"

"I did not!" said Erin. "I beat you fair and square!"

"You did not!" said Jacob. "You got a head start, and you trespassed, and you didn't wait while I tied my shoe!"

Erin tried not to laugh but she couldn't help it.

"I wonder how the lady I saw going into Aunt Kate's room could have bushy blond hair on her head and bushy brown hair on her toes," said Erin, when she stopped laughing.

"Maybe she dyed her hair so people wouldn't recognize her," said Jacob.

"And then, maybe she dyed it back today." He took off his shoes and socks and wiggled his toes in the so warm sand.

"That would mean we should be looking for someo with bushy brown hair," he continued.

"And…" Jacob paused a moment. "What if she put in a ponytail today?" He held his index finger under his ch tilted his head backwards, and scanned the blue sky abov "That would mean we need to be looking for someone with bushy brown ponytail."

"And what if she has a pet seagull that likes to ride top of her head?" Jacob lay back in the sand and moved arms back and forth like he was making a sand angel. "Th means we'd need to look for a lady with a bushy brown ponytail with a seagull on top of her head."

"And what if the seagull likes…" Jacob began to laugh.

"Okay, Jacob," said Erin. "That's enough. We're wasting time again. We have to find my mother's basket before it's too late and it's gone forever!"

"Maybe the thief wore a wig," said Jacob. He started laughing again. "Or else she dyed the hair on her toes!"

"I think you're right about the wig," said Erin. "That would explain her having blond hair on her head and brown hair on her toes." She looked at her watch and stood up. "We'll have time to go to the Atheneum before we meet Aunt Kate if we leave now," she said. "We can look for someone with bushy hair and big hairy toes, whatever color they might be, on the way."

Erin and Jacob left the beach and walked back toward tow

Just as they turned up India Street toward the Atheneum, th

saw Jane coming down the street toward them.

"Oh, Erin, I'm so sorry to hear about your mothe

lightship basket being stolen!" Jane exclaimed. "I told t

police I'd help them in any way I could!"

"Thanks, Jane," said Erin. "I'm sure they apprecia

that. I really want to find my mother's basket." She glanced

the black plastic bag Jane was carrying.

Jane tightened her grip on the bag. "I'm sorry I ca

talk right now. I need to deliver this and get back to t

Harbor House." Erin and Jacob watched as Jane walked do

India Street and took a right toward town.

"I wonder what's in the package she's carrying," said Erin. "She seemed nervous. A lightship basket would fit perfectly in that plastic bag."

"Maybe we could follow her from a distance and see where she goes," said Jacob. "I've got my binoculars."

"Good idea," said Erin. "I don't think Jane is the thief, but we can't leave any stone unturned."

Erin and Jacob followed Jane to the Boat Basin. "There she is!" said Erin, pointing. "Jane's walking down Straight Wharf."

Erin and Jacob ran to the wharf and then walked behind a group of people, keeping their distance so Jane wouldn't see them.

"She's getting on that yacht!" said Erin poking her head out from behind a large lady wearing a floppy, flowered beach hat.

59

Jacob took out his binoculars. "She reached up and took something off a ledge near the door. Now she bending over in front of the door."

"She probably just got the key to the cabin and opening the door," said Erin.

"She went inside," Jacob said.

"We could wait until Jane leaves and then get the k to the cabin and see what's inside the black bag," said Erin.

They ran down the wharf a short way and duck into a shop.

"There she goes," said Erin when she saw Ja leaving the yacht. "Let's go see what's in the black plas bag!"

"Hold on!" said Jacob. "What if we get caugh Breaking and entering is against the law!"

"It will only take a minute," said Erin. "And we won't be breaking anything. We'll just take the key off the ledge, unlock the door, see what's in the bag and then lock the door behind us when we leave."

"All right," said Jacob. "But this better be quick!"

Erin and Jacob found the key on the ledge near the cabin door, unlocked the door, and laid the key back on the ledge. "We'll lock the door when we come out," said Erin.

They found the black plastic bag lying on a bunk in the bedroom of the cabin. Inside the bag was a box of brochures about the Arts Council with Peter Anderson's name on it.

"I'm glad that's what's in the bag," said Erin. "I don't want Jane to be the thief."

"This must be Peter Anderson's yacht," said Jacob. He looked at the big wheel in the front of the cabin. "My dad

61

lets me drive the truck when we go to the farm. I bet I cou

drive a yacht, too!"

Suddenly there was a click at the door.

Erin ran to the door just in time to see Peter's niec

Adrienne, jump off the yacht and run down the wharf.

She twisted the knob on the door. "It's locked!" s

exclaimed. "It won't open!"

Jacob tried the knob. "Maybe we can get out

window," he said. He looked back at the bedroom in t

yacht. "Look! There's a sliding window with no screen. I

big enough for us to crawl through. Then we can jump o

and swim to the pier!"

"I can't swim!" said Erin.

The front door clicked again, and Erin heard voic

outside.

"Quick! Get behind that couch!" exclaimed Jacob. He and Erin crawled behind a small couch next to the bunk in the bedroom just as a man and a woman came into the cabin of the yacht.

"It's great Peter's letting us use his yacht for a little fishing," said the woman.

"Yeah, I told him we'd have it back by three o'clock for sure," answered the man.

Erin heard the engine grinding on.

She peeked out from behind the couch. Through the doorway she could see the man and woman in the front of the cabin. She and Jacob could easily run out the door but the woman was standing in front of it. The man was by the wheel.

"What are we going to do?" she whispered. "We can't stay here all day!"

"Crawl out that window and jump!" said Jacob.

Erin looked up at the window. "I can't swim!" she said again.

"Hold my hand when we jump," said Jacob, "and tread water. I'll help you to the pier!"

The driver gunned the engine and the yacht slowly moved away from the pier.

Jacob grabbed Erin's hand. "We've got to do it now before we get too far away from the wharf, unless you want to be fish food!"

Erin scrambled out the window behind Jacob, and on the count of three they splashed into the sparkling water of the Nantucket Boat Basin.

Bushy Blond Wig

"That was fun," said Jacob as they scrambled out of the water onto Straight Wharf. "I can see the newspaper headlines – FRIENDS OF RECIPIENT OF *EXCELLENCE IN SERVICE TO NANTUCKET AWARD* PRACTICE DIVING OFF YACHT IN BOAT BASIN."

"Thanks for helping me to the pier," said Erin. She noticed people staring at their wet clothes as they walked down the wharf. "It was scary to jump off the yacht into the water, but I felt safe with you holding onto my hand."

"Thanks," said Jacob. "In swim team I learned how to help someone in the water last summer. I knew I could get you to the pier if you treaded water and let me pull you along. You did a great job!"

"This wouldn't have happened if Peter Anderson's niece hadn't locked us in," said Erin.

"You mean Adrienne Smith?" said Jacob.

"Yes," said Erin. "I saw her jump off the deck and run down the wharf right after I heard the click of the door being locked. She must have done it."

"Why would she do that?" said Jacob, shaking his head to get the water out of his hair.

"I don't know," said Erin. "For some reason, I don't think she likes me." She looked at her watch. "We won't have time to go to the Atheneum now. Maybe we'll have some time after our bike ride with Aunt Kate."

67

Erin pointed to a large red vessel docked in t[he] harbor with the word NANTUCKET painted in big wh[ite] letters across the hull. "That's a lightship like the one that w[as] stationed in the South Shoals, where they made the fi[rst] lightship baskets!"

"Why did they make lightship baskets on a boat[?]" said Jacob. "Wouldn't it be easier to make them on land?"

Erin looked up and down the street before steppi[ng] off the curb onto Main Street. "Years ago, crewmen we[re] stationed on the lightships around Nantucket for seve[ral] months at a time. The crew on the lightship at the Sou[th] Shoals made baskets to pass the time and these bask[ets] became known as lightship baskets. After a while a lid w[as] added to some of the baskets and lightship baskets with l[ids] are used as purses today."

"Look," she said. She pointed to a man sitting at a table outside a shop on the corner of the street. "He's weaving a lightship basket."

Jacob peered through the shiny windows of the shop at the honey-colored baskets on display inside. "There sure are a lot of baskets in there."

"I'm glad you said that!" said Erin. She opened the door of the shop. "Wait here and keep a look out for bushy hair and hairy toes. I'll be right back."

Inside the shop Erin walked up to a woman standing behind a glass cabinet full of lightship baskets and asked to speak to the owner.

"That's me," said the woman. A miniature Nantucket lightship basket hung from around her neck. "How may I help you? It looks like you've been swimming," she added with a smile.

"Well, sort of," said Erin. She smiled back at the woman and pushed wet hair out of her face. "I wanted to see if you had any Jose Reyes lightship baskets for sale."

"I'm sorry, I don't," said the woman. "It's funny you should ask though, because a woman came in when we first opened this morning at eight o'clock and wanted to sell a very nice Jose Reyes basket, but I couldn't afford to pay what she was asking for it."

"Did she leave her name or a number where she could be reached in case you changed your mind?" asked Erin.

"No, I'm sorry, she didn't," said the woman.

"Do you remember what she was wearing?" asked Erin.

"She was wearing a black suit and dark sunglasses and had lots of bushy blond hair," said the woman.

70

Erin took a pencil and piece of paper off the counter and wrote down the name of the police officer she had talked to the night before and handed it to the woman. "Would you please call this officer at the police station if the lady comes back and wants to sell the basket again?" she said. "The police are looking for a thief who stole a Jose Reyes basket yesterday that belonged to my mother. The woman you described fits the description of the thief."

"I certainly will," said the woman. "I'll call the other lightship basket shops on Nantucket and ask them to do the same."

Erin stepped out of the shop and blinked at the bright sunlight. Jacob grabbed her arm. "I found someone with really hairy toes!" he exclaimed.

71

"Where? Where are they?" Erin looked at the feet of people waking back and forth in front of the shop.

"Right here." Jacob walked over to a man sitting on bench reading a newspaper. Then he bent down and began pet the golden retriever sitting at the man's feet. "See. He toes are really hairy, but when I asked her if she stole lightship basket, she just licked my hand and wagged her ta I don't know if that means 'yes' or 'no' but I think she's w too nice to be a thief."

The man reading the newspaper smiled at Erin as s bent down to pet the dog. "What a sweet dog!" she said the dog licked her face. "You *are* too nice of a dog to b thief!"

When Erin and Jacob arrived at the Harbor House they had a message at the front desk to call Aunt Kate.

"Aunt Kate's car needs a new part before she can drive back to Nantucket from 'Sconset, so she won't be here for our bike ride around the island," Erin said, covering the phone with her hand while she talked to Jacob. "She'll be back around five. She said Jane wanted to know if we'd like to help serve hors d'oeuvres at a benefit she and Peter are hosting for the Nantucket Arts Council at the Harbor House pool this evening at six. They'd only need us for an hour or so. The waitresses would take over and serve dinner after that."

"That sounds like fun," said Jacob. "We might make some tips. And we'd probably have to sample the hor d'oeuvres so we can recommend the good ones." He grinned.

"Aunt Kate said she promised Jane and Peter th[at] she'd attend the dinner at the pool and Peter's presentati[on] afterward," said Erin, still covering the phone while s[he] talked. "We can eat in the Hearth Restaurant after we fini[sh] serving, and when Aunt Kate is through at the pool, you a[nd] I and Aunt Kate and Uncle Dave can walk downtown f[or] fudge and see the Boat Basin at night. It's really pretty then.

"Count me in," said Jacob. "I never pass up fudge!"

"Now we'll have plenty of time to go to the Atheneum af[ter] lunch since we don't have to serve until six," said Erin as s[he] and Jacob chose a table in the Hearth Restaurant. "I re[ally] want to have a nice presentation for Aunt Kate and find [out] more about my family."

"I'll be right back," Erin said, after the waitress had taken their order. "I want to go downstairs and see the housekeeping department where my dad and mom worked, since the Harbor House won't be the same after this summer."

"Here, take my camera. You might want to take some pictures," said Jacob.

The door to the housekeeping department was open, but there was no one there when Erin walked into the spacious, rectangular room. A large desk with a lamp and stacks of neatly arranged papers sat in one corner of the room. Sheets, pillow cases, blankets, bedspreads, towels, wash cloths, soap and shampoo were stacked on shelves that ran around three sides of the room. Lockers with names of housekeepers on them stood on a fourth wall.

Just as she raised Jacob's camera to take a pictur

Erin saw something yellow on top of one of the lockers o

of the corner of her eye. She walked over to take a clos

look and saw that it was a bushy blond wig.

"Can we help you?" Two housekeepers in Harb

House uniforms smiled at Erin as she turned around.

"Oh, no, thank you," said Erin. "I was just stoppi

by to see the housekeeping department. My father used to

the executive housekeeper at the Harbor House." She point

to the wig on top of the locker. "I wondered if you kn

who the yellow wig on top of that locker belonged to. I

been looking for one like that."

"Oh," said one of the girls. "That belongs to Micha

He wore it for a Halloween party here at the Harbor Hou

last fall. It's been lying around ever since."

"Does he still work here?" said Erin.

"Yes," said the other girl. "He's working up on the third floor today. We start at nine in the morning and finish at three in the afternoon."

Erin thanked the two girls and ran up the stairs to the table in the Hearth Restaurant.

"Did you take some pictures?" asked Jacob.

"No," said Erin. She handed Jacob his camera. "But I saw a bushy blond wig on top of one of the lockers!" she exclaimed. "It belongs to a housekeeper named Michael who is working up on the third floor right now. I'm going up there now to get a look at him. If that's his wig, he could be the thief!"

Jacob told the waitress they'd be back and followed Erin up the stairs.

A housekeeper with curly brown hair was taking towels from a cart into Jacob's room just as they reached the

third floor. Erin noticed he was about the same height as t[...]
woman she had seen going into Aunt Kate's room.

"Does he look like the thief?" whispered Jacob.

"He's the same size," said Erin. She hoped he was t[...]
thief. She was ready to solve this crime and get her mothe[...]
lightship basket back.

"Why don't we go in and ask him for some ex[...]
towels?" Jacob suggested. "Then you could check his to[...]
We can always use extra towels if we go to the beach."

"Hello! May I help you?" The housekeeper gree[...]
Erin and Jacob when they entered the room. He had j[...]
finished making Jacob's bed. Erin introduced herself a[...]
Jacob and said they were guests of Aunt Kate's next door a[...]
wondered if they could have some extra towels.

"My name is Michael," the young man said. "I'd[...]
happy to help you." Erin glanced at the housekeeper's feet[...]

he got some towels off the cart in the hallway but he was wearing tennis shoes and she couldn't see his toes.

Michael laid the towels down on Jacob's bed. "Please let me know if there's anything else you need."

"This room looks great," said Jacob. "You could clean my room at home anytime!"

"Thanks! You can give me a tip if you want when you leave," Michael said smiling. "There's an envelope on the dresser."

"Do you work here every day?" asked Jacob.

"Every day from nine to three during the summer," said Michael. "I don't take any days off because I'm saving money for college in the fall."

Erin and Jacob said good-bye to Michael and walked downstairs.

"Michael seems to be a really nice a guy," said Jacob. "Too nice of a guy to be a thief."

"I think Michael *could* be the thief," said Erin, "even though I couldn't see his toes. He's the same size as the woman I saw going into Aunt Kate's room. And he would have had plenty of time to go to the lightship basket shop at eight this morning and be at work at the Harbor House at nine. Plus, he needs money for school."

"We could follow him when he gets off from work," said Jacob. "If he's the thief, he might try to sell Aunt Kate's basket again."

"That's an idea," said Erin. "We could go to the Atheneum after lunch as we planned and rent bikes on the way back. That way, if Michael uses a bike to get around, we can still follow him."

Dirty, Dusty, Bushy Blond Wig

Erin gave the reference books she'd been using to t
librarian in the reference room of the Atheneum and walk
over to the table where Jacob was looking at a book abc
whales. She'd gotten the information she needed about Au
Kate's donations to organizations on Nantucket and a
information about the Delaney family. She just had one mc
thing to do.

"Want to come with me?" Erin whispered. "I want
see if the librarian knows anything about the news release y
found in the scrapbook at the Harbor House about the th
from the Smith's residence. I found out my great-grandfath

Patrick Delaney, and his family lived at 16 India Street in 1952. That's right next door to 18 India Street where the Smith's lived in 1952."

"I don't think there is any more written information about the theft," said the reference librarian in a quiet voice. "But I remember my great-grandparents and my grandparents talking about it. Some islanders thought Patrick Delaney stole the safe. But other islanders said that Patrick Delaney could never be the thief because he was an outstanding citizen and too good of a person to do anything like that." She got up to help a patron and then returned to her seat.

"The Smiths had planned to use the money in the safe to start a bed and breakfast but they couldn't do it once the safe was stolen," she continued. "The Smiths always thought Patrick Delaney stole the safe because a neighbor had seen someone running from the house the night of t

robbery and said he resembled Patrick Delaney, but it was

very dark night and the neighbor couldn't be sure who it w

Mr. Delaney denied any involvement in the theft."

She stopped to answer her phone.

"People all over the island gossiped about the th

and a feud developed between the Smith and Delan

families," the librarian said after she finished her call. "T

Smith children and the Delaney children never got along a

were always fighting."

"Did they ever find the thief?" Erin asked.

'No," said the librarian. "They never found the th

or the safe. Soon after the theft Patrick Delaney and

family opened a very successful bed and breakfast here

Nantucket. They sold it in 1990, but it's still in operat

today," she said.

"I remember my father saying something about that," said Erin.

"The Smiths thought the Delaneys used the money they stole to start the business," continued the librarian. "Ever since the theft, members of the Delaney family have been accused of various thefts of jewelry and valuables on the island, but it's never been proved that any of them actually committed any of the crimes," she said.

"I can see why the Smiths were feuding with the Delaneys if they thought Patrick Delaney stole all the money and jewels they had saved to start a business," said Jacob as they walked down the steps of the Atheneum, "and then used the money to start a business of their own. Maybe some of them are still feuding."

"I think Adrienne is," said Erin. "She probably doesn't like me because I'm a Delaney. I can't think of any other reason why she'd lock the door to the yacht when 〈…〉 were inside."

"Uncle Dave is a Delaney," said Jacob. "Maybe 〈…〉 Smith framed Uncle Dave because some of the Smiths did 〈…〉 want him to get the job at the Grey Whale Hotel."

"You might be right about that," said Erin. "No o〈…〉 would hire Uncle Dave as the manager of a hotel if th〈…〉 thought he stole jewelry from one of the guests."

"And maybe the housekeeper you saw going i〈…〉 Aunt Kate's room was a still-feuding Smith who decided 〈…〉 steal the basket because the Smiths thought they deserve〈…〉 since they thought your great-grandfather stole a bunch 〈…〉 money from them."

He picked up a shell in the road and tossed it into 〈…〉 grass. "Hey, wait a minute," he said, stopping in the middle 〈…〉 the road. "Remember when Jane said they called Mary S t〈…〉

because her last name was Mary Smith? Maybe *she* took your mother's basket!"

Erin thought a moment. "She could have," she said. "She probably overheard Aunt Kate saying she'd meet us for dinner at six. Practically everyone on the island knows Aunt Kate's been keeping my mother's basket for me. Mary S could have easily made a copy of the key to Aunt Kate's room and used it to open the door."

Erin opened the door to the bike shop. "I think both Marys will be working tonight because of the benefit. We can find out where Mary S lives and if it's not too far we can walk to her house after we finish serving the hors d'oeuvres. Since people on the island aren't too careful about locking their doors or hiding their keys, maybe we can walk in quickly and see if we see the basket."

At three o'clock Erin and Jacob looked for Michael out t
windows of the Harbor House lobby.

"Hey, look," said Jacob. "There's Adrienne by the bi
rack. She's bending down doing something."

Erin ran out the front door of the Harbor Hou
toward the bike rack. "What are you doing?" she demanded

Adrienne stood up quickly. "Nothing," she sa
"Besides, what business is it of yours?"

"Why did you lock us in Peter's yacht?" asked E
taking a step closer to Adrienne.

"I didn't lock you in Peter's yacht. I didn't even kn
you were there," said Adrienne.

"I saw you jump off the yacht and run down
wharf when the door was locked," said Erin.

"Excuse me. I have to talk to my aunt," said Adrienne, walking to the front door of the Harbor House.

Erin and Jacob ducked behind a bush beside the Harbor House and waited until Michael came around the side of the building, pulled a bike out of the bike rack, and began riding toward town.

Erin and Jacob jumped on their bikes.

"My tires are flat!" exclaimed Erin.

"So are mine," said Jacob. "They were fine when we put them in the rack. Someone must have let the air out of them!"

"I think I know who let the air out of them," said Erin. She got off her bike. "If we run, we can catch up with Michael, at least for a while. You can't ride very fast on cobblestoned streets or sidewalks filled with people."

Erin and Jacob watched as Michael got off his bi[ke]
three blocks later, looked back at the way he had come a[nd]
then turned into an alleyway right before he reached M[ain]
Street.

Erin and Jacob ran and turned down the alleyway b[ut]
there was no sign of Michael.

"Where did he go?" said Jacob.

"There's his bike," said Erin, pointing to a bike i[n] a
rack near the entrance to a store a short way down [the]
alleyway.

"I think Michael recognized us when he turn[ed]
around," said Erin. "And now he's trying to lose us [by]
ditching his bike here and going out the front door of [the]
store." She grabbed Jacob's arm. "Quick!" she said. "If [we]
hurry, we can see which way he goes."

Jacob followed Erin as she ran out of the alleyway and up to Main Street.

"I don't see him," said Jacob as they walked down Main Street.

"Wait! Look! There he is!" Jacob pointed through the window of a store that said Nantucket Pharmacy.

"Hi!" said Michael when Erin and Jacob walked in the store. He was wearing a black baseball cap and apron and standing behind a counter in the front of the store making ice cream cones for people waiting in line. "I saw you on my way here. Would you like a free sample of ice cream?"

"Sure," said Jacob.

"Do you work here every day?" he asked, when Michael handed him a small cone of chocolate ice cream.

"Every day except Sundays until seven o'clock."

"Michael seems to be a very busy, nice guy," said Jacob on their way back to the Harbor House. "Too nice and too busy to be a thief!"

"I'm going downstairs and look at that wig on top of Michael's locker," said Erin after she and Jacob arrived at the Harbor House. "I never really saw it up close. I still think Michael could be the thief. Just because he's nice and busy doesn't mean he wouldn't steal a lightship basket."

The housekeeping department was empty when Erin walked into the room. Jacob kept watch at the door while Erin climbed up a small ladder and pulled a bushy blond wig off the top of Michael's locker.

"EW-w-w," she said, holding the wig at arm's length as she came down the ladder.

Jacob looked in the door. The wig was full of dust and dirt and spider webs. "It doesn't look like anyone has worn that for a while!" he said. "Or, would want to!"

A Close Call

Erin and Jacob found out from Uncle Dave that Ma

S lived on Hulbert Avenue outside of town and decided to

to find a way to get there the following day to check for ﬞ

basket.

When they arrived at the pool, guests stood talking

groups and relaxing in lounge chairs. Some swam in the po

A bartender was stationed at a refreshment bar decora

with balloons and streamers. Erin smoothed the shirt of ﬞ

black and white server outfit Jane had given her. She laugl

at Jacob's matching outfit. "We look like real waiters,"

said.

"Hey, I can do this," said Jacob, picking up a tray of little tuna fish sandwiches. "It's like balancing your lunch tray at school!"

"Offer some to each person," said the bartender. "But don't eat any. You'll get us all fired," he said with a wink.

Erin picked up a tray of crackers topped with cheese and olives from the countertop and walked to where Aunt Kate, Jane, and Peter Anderson were sitting. "I've picked two of your pictures for the art show," said Peter, taking an hors d'oeuvres from Erin's tray. "Your drawings are quite good."

"Thank you!" said Erin. "I'm really excited to be in the show!"

"That's a compliment coming from Peter Anderson!" said Jane.

"It certainly is!" said Aunt Kate. "Peter is a wonderful artist! It's in his genes. With a famous artist like Peter Smith for a great-grandfather, what else could he be?"

"Is Peter Smith your real name?" asked Erin, looking at Peter. She could hardly believe her ears.

"No, my real name is Peter Anderson," said Peter. "My mother was a Smith and my great-grandparents and grandparents were all Smiths, so I'm a member of the Smith family. But my mother married an Anderson so Anderson is my last name."

"Did your great-grandfather live at 18 India Street?" asked Erin.

"Yes, he did," said Peter. "I remember playing there when I was a little boy."

A minute later Erin pulled Jacob back to the refreshment stand. "Change of plans," she said. She set empty hors d'oeuvres tray down on the counter and picked up a full one.

Jacob wrinkled his forehead. "What do you mean change of plans?" he asked. "Hey, before you tell me what you mean, what's the best way to get a sandwich out of the pool?"

"I found out that Peter Anderson's great-grandfather was Peter Smith, who lived at 18 India Street and was a famous artist here on the island," said Erin, ignoring Jacob's question. "Peter is a member of the Smith family even though his last name is Anderson." With a napkin, she wiped some cheese off the side of the tray she was carrying. "I couldn't see his toes, but I saw Jane's and she's not the thief."

"That's interesting," said Jacob.

"Since Peter's going to be giving a presentation here during dinner, I think we should go check his house and look for the basket," Erin continued. "We know how to get in. V

could still be back in time to walk downtown with Aunt K

and Uncle Dave."

When they reached Peter's house, Erin took the key fr

under the statue and unlocked the door, then carefu

returned the key to its hiding place. "We can lock the d

behind us when we're finished searching," she said.

"Hey, I wonder what's in the fridge!" said Jacob wh

they were in the house. "A little snack always helps wh

you're looking for stolen property!"

"We can't goof around," said Erin. "We have to m

Aunt Kate and Uncle Dave after Peter's presentation—p

doing this gives me the heebie-jeebies. I just want to

finished and get out!"

"Let's look behind the furniture and in closets first." Erin bent over and looked behind a striped rose and brown couch. "A lightship basket would fit perfectly behind a couch or in the back of a closet."

Jacob opened the door to a big walk-in closet. Clothes hanging on rods covered the side walls and shelves that reached the ceiling covered the back wall. "It could be in here," he said, walking into the closet. "Boy, this dude sure has some weird-looking clothes!" he said.

Erin came over and walked in the closet behind Jacob.

Suddenly the front door opened. "Who's here? Is somebody here?" Peter's voice floated toward them from the entry way.

"Quick!" whispered Jacob. "Shut the closet door!"

"What's the matter, Peter?" Jane's voice followed Peter's.

"The door was unlocked. The key was under t' statue, but the door was unlocked. I always lock it when leave."

"You were probably just in a hurry to get to t' benefit and not thinking about what you were doing. Hu' now! We've got to find that poster you made and show t' members or you may not be getting any donations at all!"

Erin could tell from the sound of their voices t' Jane and Peter were both in the living room now. Her he' was racing a mile a minute.

"I know it's here somewhere," said Peter. "I j' finished it this afternoon. It's not on the drawing table or ' easel," he said.

The knob on the closet door turned. The d' opened and light flooded the closet.

"Maybe I put it in the closet," said Peter. "Sometimes I put things in here so they won't get damaged." He began to shift the clothes back and forth on the rods near the door.

Erin crouched behind a long, woolen coat. The bottom of the coat reached the floor and hid her feet. She

could feel the coat moving as Peter came closer, shifting the clothes back and forth so he could see behind them.

"Oh, look! Here it is," said Jane.

"Where?" said Peter.

"Here, standing up behind the couch," said Jane.

"Oh, now I remember putting it there," said Peter.
wanted to make sure nothing happened to it."

"Let's go so we can get back in time for t
presentation," said Jane. "Remember to lock the door t
time."

The closet door closed and everything went d
again.

Lunch with a Thief

Erin and Jacob stood in the darkness after Peter and Jane shut the front door behind them. Erin took a few deep breaths. *What would they have said if Peter and Jane had found them in the closet? We thought you might have stolen my mother's lightship basket, so we thought we'd come and take a look? What would Aunt Kate think?* She peered out into the darkness from behind the coat. "I think they're gone," she whispered and felt her way to the door.

Light flooded the inside of the closet when she opened the door.

Jacob came out from behind a long curtain hangi near the back of the closet. "That was close," he said.

"It's a good thing there were so many clothes to hi behind in here. Look at this," he said. He bent down a picked up a blond wig off the floor. "I think I knocked it the shelf when I was getting behind the curtain."

Erin took the wig out of Jacob's hand. Her heart w still thumping wildly in her chest. "This looks like the hair the housekeeper I saw going into Aunt Kate's room," s said.

"Peter probably wore it for Halloween like Michae or maybe for a play. Peter's in the arts, you know," said Jaco

Erin handed the wig back to Jacob. "You're rig Peter could have worn this wig for Halloween or for a p but he could also have used it to disguise himself a housekeeper and steal my mother's lightship basket."

Suddenly the phone rang. When no one answered, a voice left a message on the answering machine. "Meet me at the Ropewalk Restaurant tomorrow at one o'clock," it said. "I'll have the money."

"It sounds like Peter is going to sell something," said Erin. She thought for a moment. "Maybe Peter is a still-feuding Smith who stole my mother's basket and is going to sell it to someone else. I think we should check out the Ropewalk Restaurant tomorrow and see what Peter is selling. I can't let my mother's lightship basket get away forever!"

"Sounds good to me!" said Jacob. "But let's get out of here before they come back!"

At 12:45 pm the following day Erin and Jacob stood insi

the entrance to the Ropewalk Restaurant. Rows of windo

overlooking the harbor wound around the room.

"My mother wouldn't recognize me dressed like thi

said Jacob. "I can see why the Thrift Shop sells this stuff fo

dollar a bag!" He yanked a baseball cap down over the cu

brown wig he was wearing and adjusted blue sunglasses t

kept sliding off his nose.

"You *do* look ridiculous, but at least it's for a go

cause." Erin's blond hair was tucked up under a red be

hat. Red hoops dangled from her ears. She wore sunglas

with white and red striped frames and a pink backpack hu

from her shoulders. "It's a quarter to one. Pretend we

waiting for someone and keep a lookout for Peter. Keep your sunglasses on so we won't be recognized."

A tall man in shorts and a Nantucket t-shirt came in with three young children in swimming suits and sat at a table near the front of the room. Then two teen-aged girls wearing rhinestone-studded sunglasses and cut-off jeans sat down at a table not far from the man with the children. An older man with a walking cane and his wife came in and sat at the oyster bar. By 1:30 pm more people had entered the restaurant and others had left, but there was no sign of Peter. Erin wondered if he was coming and if they'd ever find her mother's basket.

"Why don't we take a table and get something to eat while we're waiting," she said. "Just keep a lookout for anyone that looks like Peter Anderson."

Erin and Jacob took a table near the entrance to the restaurant and ordered two large bowls of chowder.

"Oh!" said Erin after the waitress had brought the order. She pointed to a table up from theirs where Peter and another man had just taken seats.

"Look," said Jacob. The man laid an envelope on the table. Peter picked it up, looked inside, and put it in his pocket. Then he picked up a sports bag from under his chair and slid it across the table to the man. The man unzipped the bag, looked inside, and nodded before stashing the bag under his own chair.

"It looks as if Peter sold him whatever is in the sports bag," said Jacob.

"I've got to get that bag and look inside," said Erin. "If Peter is the thief, he may have just sold my mother's basket to that man."

"They're going to the oyster bar," said Jacob.

"Can you do something to distract them while I check the bag?" said Erin. "I'll meet you outside after I check it."

"You better believe I can!" said Jacob. "Distraction is right up my alley!" He picked up their bowls of chowder and walked toward the oyster bar. As he approached the oyster bar, he pretended to trip and lunged forward, sending chowder flying out of the bowls onto Peter and the man.

"What's going on!" yelled the man, jumping off his stool. Chowder dripped down his shirt and pants and onto the floor under his stool.

Jacob grabbed a chowder-soaked napkin off the bar and began wiping chowder off the man's shirt. "I'm so sorry!" he said.

"Can't you see!" hissed Peter. He had chowder down the back of his jacket and in his hair.

"Let me help you!" Jacob began wiping off the ba

of Peter's jacket with the napkin.

Erin crawled over to Peter's table, grabbed the b

from under the table, and unzipped it. Inside was a sm

painting like the ones she had seen in Peter's gallery.

Quickly Erin pressed on the picture and it moved sideways in the frame, exposing a compartment built into the frame back with a small, velvet draw-string pouch in it. Erin opened the pouch and looked inside it. Then she quickly returned the pouch, put the painting in her backpack and ran out of the restaurant.

"Did you find the basket?" said Jacob as they ripped off their disguises and stuffed them into Erin's backpack as they ran toward the Harbor House.

"No basket," she said. "But there was a picture like the ones I saw at Peter's gallery with the little compartment in it and it had diamonds in it."

"Wow!" exclaimed Jacob. "Those might have been stolen diamonds."

"I know," said Erin. "That's why I brought them along to show the police."

"You've got to be kidding!" exclaimed Jacob. "No you're a thief!"

"No, I'm not," said Erin. "I'm going to give them the police so they can see if they're stolen. If they're n maybe the police will give the painting back to Peter but 1 tell him where they got it."

Going for a Ride?

Mary F pulled her bike out of the bike rack just as Erin and Jacob arrived at the Harbor House.

"Are you going home already?" asked Jacob when he saw her.

"No. I'm just taking a quick ride out Hulbert Avenue to pick up some allergy medicine," said Mary F. "I'll be right back. Would you all like to come along?"

"We'd love to," said Erin. *Maybe we can find out where Mary S lives* she thought.

"We heard about Hulbert Avenue and were wondering where it was," said Jacob.

113

Erin and Jacob followed Mary F as she rode out

town toward Brant Point and then turned left on a road w

views of Nantucket Sound on the right hand side of t

road.

"What a beautiful house," exclaimed Erin as Mary

turned off Hulbert Avenue onto the driveway of a large tw

story house with a wrap-around porch and a rose garden

the front yard.

"It belongs to my aunt and uncle," said Mary

"They're away for several months and are letting me stay h

for the summer while I work at the Harbor House to m:

money for college. My cousin Mary S lives here and so d

my niece, Adrienne. We're taking care of her while

parents are away for the summer also."

After they parked their bikes in the bike rack, Mar

led the way up a gravel path to the house. She sneezed th

times as she passed the rose garden. "I seem to have an allergy to everything," she said, "including roses. It's a good thing I'm studying nursing in school. Maybe I'll find a cure for allergies."

She pushed open a side door to the house and led the way through an entryway into the kitchen. "You can sit here for a minute if you like," she said. "I just need to run upstairs."

"Well, now we know how to get to Mary S's," said Jacob, looking around the spacious kitchen.

"Yes, we do," said Erin, "but I don't think she stole the lightship basket."

"What do you mean?"

"I'll tell you later," said Erin as Mary F came back downstairs.

Mary F pulled out a chair, grabbed a pair of sho

from the entryway, switched the pair she was wearing with t

pair from the entryway, and then stood up.

"I wish I had enough time to give you a tour," s

said, leading the way back outside to the bikes, "but I have

get back to the Harbor House if I want to keep my job!"

"We've got to go back to Mary F's house and look for

basket," said Erin, after she and Jacob thanked Mary F for

ride and she went inside the Harbor House.

"Why? You said you didn't think Mary S was

thief."

Erin straddled her bike as she turned it around on

road in front of the Harbor House.

"I think Mary F is the thief," she said. "She sneezes just the way the housekeeper did who I saw going into Aunt Kate's room, and her toes look the same. I saw them when she changed her shoes. If she's the thief, the basket might be somewhere in the house."

Erin rode out the entrance to the Harbor House and turned left.

"Plus, I left my backpack with the painting in it in the kitchen at Mary F's house. I need to get it back."

"You must have left it there on purpose." Jacob rode behind Erin as she led the way out of town. "That's not something you'd forget by accident."

"I did leave it on purpose," said Erin, waiting for a car to pass before continuing through an intersection. "I saw Mary S working this morning so she shouldn't be there and Mary F just went back to work. But if anyone *is* there, we can say we came for my backpack and leave. And if there's no o

there, we can look for the basket."

"But what if someone finds the painting with t

diamonds inside it?"

"They won't," said Erin. "I put the diamonds in t

zip-up pocket of my shorts before we left the house."

Erin found her backpack on the floor by the table where

left it with the painting still in it.

"Where would you hide a stolen lightship baske

she said, threading her arms through the straps of

backpack.

"Maybe in a closet or the basement," said Jacob.

Erin looked at her watch. "It's three o'clock,"

said. "Let's check the closets upstairs first. If we don't f the basket upstairs, we can check the closets here on the first floor and then check the basement. I want to get out of here as fast as we can."

After they hadn't found Aunt Kate's basket in the closets upstairs or on the first floor, Erin and Jacob went back to the kitchen.

"I bet this is the basement," said Jacob. He opened a door that led down carpeted steps to a large room with a leather couch and matching chairs. Sunshine poured in through windows that lined the walls and a glass door led to a patio with blooming flowers in pots and lawn chairs. There were bookshelves and cabinets along the walls in between the windows.

Erin opened the doors to a cabinet full of books about Nantucket and whales. "No basket here," she said. She looked in another cabinet, but it was full of more books a

some games.

"I wonder what this is for?" said Jacob. He pushed

button inside the back wall of a cabinet and a door to a sm

room next to the cabinet opened.

Inside the room was a workbench strewn with

hammer, nails, pieces of wood, and a saw on one side a

several small paintings like the ones Erin had seen in Pete

gallery on the other. A small pile of diamonds lay next to

paintings.

"It looks like someone is putting diamonds

paintings," said Jacob. He opened a cabinet.

"Hey! Look!" he said, pointing to three lights

baskets on the bottom shelf of the cabinet. "Lights

baskets!"

All three baskets had whale carvings on the lid. Erin quickly checked the bottom of each basket. "I can't believe it!" she said, when she saw the bottom of the third basket. "It's my mother's!"

"Quick! Let's get out of here!" said Jacob. He pushed the button in the cabinet to close the door to the workroom and they raced up the stairs.

Mary S stood in the doorway at the top of the stairs. "What are you doing here?" she said. She glared at Erin.

"We wanted to see if Mary F wanted to take a bike ride," Erin lied.

"She's not here," said Mary S. "She's at work."

"I guess we'd better be going then," said Erin, pushing her way around Mary S and into the kitchen.

"Not so fast!" said Mary S. She spied the bask[et]
behind Erin's back and grabbed it, but Erin held on tig[ht.]
"Where did you get this basket?"

"It's mine!" Erin exclaimed. "It belonged to [my]
mother!"

Erin wrestled the basket free from Mary S's gra[sp.]
Mary S slipped and fell onto the kitchen floor.

"Run, Erin!" yelled Jacob, following her out [the]
kitchen door.

"Jake! Bart!" screamed Mary S behind them.

"Our bikes are gone!" exclaimed Erin when t[hey]
reached the bike rack.

"We can run down to the road and flag down a c[ar,]
said Jacob. "Somebody will see us!"

Suddenly a tall man with a beard and a short fat man wearing a baseball cap dashed out of the house toward them.

"Stop! Come back!" they hollered.

Erin and Jacob could hear the men's big shoes stomping down the driveway just before they felt their big hands grab them from behind.

"Don't worry! We'll take you on a nice ride!" said the tall man.

"Help! Let us go!" screamed Erin as the two men pulled her and Jacob up the driveway to a shed around back of the house. She dragged her feet and tried to break the tall man's grasp on her arm, but it didn't keep him from pulling her toward the shed.

Jacob kicked at the short fat man. "Let us go," hollered. "We didn't do anything!"

The men tied Erin and Jacob up with rope from the shed and put gags over their mouths. Erin looked at the tall man as he put the gag around her mouth but he did not look at her. She noticed that the hair on his bony fingers matched the color of the hair in his beard.

The men put Erin and Jacob in the bed of a shiny red pickup truck and laid a tarp over them. Then they got in the truck, shut the doors, and turned on the engine.

Erin heard the doors to the truck open and shut again.

The tall man's voice filtered through the tarp. "Don't go anywhere," he said. "We'll be right back."

New Friends

It was dark under the tarp. The engine in the truck was still running. Erin and Jacob tried to wiggle out of the ropes around their wrists and ankles, but the knots were tied too tightly.

Erin couldn't believe they were tied up in the bed of the truck with a tarp over them and no one knew where they were. She felt sorry for Jacob. If it wasn't for her, he wouldn't be tied up in the back of a pickup truck with a gag in his mouth.

Suddenly the tarp was pulled aside and Adrien climbed into the bed of the truck.

She took a knife out of her pocket and quickly cut the ropes around Erin and Jacob's wrists and ankles and took off their gags.

"Quick!" she said. "We'll take the back way to Hulbert Avenue and run to town!"

As they jumped out of the bed of the truck, they heard the voices of the two men.

"Get in the truck and lock the doors and roll up the windows!" exclaimed Jacob as the two men came running toward the truck.

"Stop!" the men cried. They pulled on the door handles, banged on the windows, and then jumped into the bed of the truck as Jacob stepped on the gas and drove around to the front of the house and down the driveway to Hulbert Avenue.

Four police cars with sirens blaring met them at t

entrance to Hulbert Avenue. When they heard the sirens a

saw the police cars, the two men jumped out of the truck a

ran up a hill into some bushes. Erin, Jacob, and Adrien

watched as five policemen ran into the bushes after them.

Then a policeman climbed into the truck and drove

off to the side of the road.

"Who called the police?" said Erin when they were

out of the truck. She watched as two police cars drove up

driveway to the house.

"Yeah!" said Jacob. "How did you know we w

here?"

"I believe this young lady had something to do w

it," said the officer looking at Adrienne.

Adrienne glanced at Erin and Jacob and hung

head. "I know I treated you badly when you first arrived

128

I'm sorry," she said. "When I saw you being tied up and put in the truck, I knew something very bad was going on and called the police. I hope you'll forgive me for the way I acted. I never want to be involved in a feud again!"

"Thanks, Adrienne," said Erin. "We forgive you!"

"You might have prevented us from being fish food," said Jacob.

That evening Jacob, Uncle Dave, and Aunt Kate went with Erin to turn over the pouch of diamonds to the police.

The police officer handed Erin her mother's lightship basket. "Thank you," she said. "Did Mary F steal it?"

"Yes, she did," said the officer, "and Mary S helped her. Members of the Delaney family stopped feuding many years ago and so did most members of the Smith family. But some members of the Smith family still think Patrick Delan[ey]

stole their safe with the money and jewels in it and feel th[ey]

can steal things from the Delaneys or frame them for crim[es]

they didn't commit. These Smiths steal diamonds and jewe[ls]

from around the island and frame the Delaneys for the the[ft.]

Then Peter Anderson sells the diamonds and jewelry in [the]

paintings to people off island, and everyone splits [the]

money."

"I'm sorry to hear Peter was involved," said A[unt]

Kate. "I've enjoyed working with him over the years."

"Who stole the diamonds from the lady at the Har[bor]

House?" said Jacob

"No one," said the officer. "The lady who accu[sed]

Uncle Dave of stealing diamonds from her room didn't h[ave]

any diamonds stolen at all. She was a member of the Sm[ith]

family trying to frame Uncle Dave so he wouldn't be hired as the manager at the Grey Whale Hotel."

"That's nice to know," said Uncle Dave. "Now maybe I'll get the job at the Grey Whale after all!"

"Are Jake and Bart feuding Smiths?" asked Erin.

"Yes, they are," said the officer.

The next morning Erin, Jacob, Adrienne, Aunt Kate, and Uncle Dave stood in line filling their plates at the breakfast buffet in the Hearth Restaurant. Adrienne was staying in Erin's room until her parents came back to the island.

After they were seated at their table, Aunt Kate held up five tickets. "Eat a big breakfast," she said. "We're all going on a whale-watching excursion when we're finished."

"Yippee!" said Jacob. "Now I can take lots of pictur of whales and put them in a new section of my scrapbo called *Giant Animals of Nantucket*!"

Erin thought a minute. "How about creating a secti in your scrapbook called *New Friends on Nantucket*?" S handed Jacob's camera to Aunt Kate. "Will you take picture, please?"

Erin draped one arm around Jacob, and the ot around Adrienne. "Say big hairy toes!" exclaimed Jacob.

Laughing, Aunt Kate clicked the picture of the th smiling friends.

Made in the USA
Middletown, DE
02 December 2020